Rapunzel

Written by Ian Beck

Illustrated by Alessandra Cimatoribus

Chapter 1

Once there was a husband and wife. They were very poor and life had always been tough.

One day, the wife told her husband that she was going to have a baby.

As the baby grew inside her, she wanted to eat fresh food, especially lettuce. The problem was that they'd no spare money to buy any.

Next door to their house, there was a large garden. The garden was owned by a rich old lady called Ma Gothel. She grew all kinds of fresh vegetables, including lettuce.

One night, the man climbed over Ma Gothel's wall and took some of her lettuce. He went back the next night and stole some more. On the third night, he went back again, but this time Ma Gothel was hiding in the dark and she caught him.

"Thief!" she called out angrily. She grabbed him hard by the arm.
"How dare you steal from me!"

"My wife was hungry and we've no money," the man stammered.

"So you thought you'd take something that isn't yours?"
Ma Gothel said.

"We're not only poor. My wife's expecting a baby, and she asked me
to get her some lettuce."

4

"A baby," said Ma Gothel, and she let go of the man's arm. "I had a child once," she said sadly, "and I lost her. I'll let you go, and I'll even give you lots of lettuce for your wife – on one condition. When your baby is born, you must give the child to me to bring up."

"I don't think my wife will let you have our baby," the man said.

"But I'm rich and you're poor. I can give your baby everything. Can *you*? Come back tomorrow night with your answer."

The next night, it was almost midnight when the man climbed over Ma Gothel's wall. She was waiting for him.

"We agree," the man said quietly, with his head bowed.

Ma Gothel smiled. She'd been lonely for a long time, but now she'd have a child to keep her company.

A few months later, the man's wife gave birth to a baby girl. She was wrapped in a blanket and handed over to Ma Gothel. The couple were too sad to stay, so they left the village that same night and no one ever saw them again.

Chapter 2

Ma Gothel named the girl Rapunzel. She had unusually long golden hair, and although she was very pretty she was also wild.

She liked nothing better than to play games outside whenever she could with the rough village boys. She especially liked playing with Ned, the farmer's son.

Ma Gothel wanted to keep Rapunzel all to herself. She didn't like her playing with Ned or any other rough child, and did her best to stop her. But Rapunzel would always find a way to escape from Ma Gothel.

Finally, when Rapunzel turned 12, Ma Gothel could stand it no longer, and she moved Rapunzel far away from the village.

Outside the village was a large forest. In the middle of the forest was a tall tower. Ma Gothel put Rapunzel in a room at the top of the tall tower, and kept her hidden away among the trees. The tower had only one door and it was kept firmly locked and bolted.

Rapunzel wasn't happy being locked away. As the years passed, she'd stand at the high window of the tower and look out at the world beyond the forest. Rapunzel was also lonely – she wanted to play with her friends from the village, but there was no way out.

The only thing Rapunzel could do was brush her long hair. And while she brushed, she sang all the old folk songs that Ned, the farmer's son, had once taught her.

Rapunzel's hair had grown so long she could plait it and lower it like a thick rope right down as far as the ground below the tower. Every evening, when Ma Gothel returned from her work in the garden, she'd call out, "Rapunzel, Rapunzel, let down your hair."

Rapunzel would lower her hair all the way down from the top of the tower to the ground below. Ma Gothel would then tie the end of the hair round her waist and Rapunzel would pull her up from the ground along with her basket. Ma Gothel could've opened the tower door, but she didn't like climbing the steep stairs.

As the years went by, Rapunzel grew more and more unhappy. She wanted to be outside in the sun, laughing with her friends, not shut up in a cold, stone tower.

Chapter 3

One morning in early summer, Ned, the farmer's son, was out riding in the forest. While Rapunzel had been locked in the tower, Ned had grown up in the village. He loved riding in the forest, but he'd never come this far before. Suddenly, he heard the sound of singing echoing through the bright leaves.

He rode towards the voice,
and after a while he found
the tall tower, which stuck up
above the trees. Someone was
singing in a room at the very top.
As Ned listened, he realised
the song sounded familiar.
It was a song about pirates
and Ned remembered it.
He'd taught that song
to Rapunzel!

He tied Dobbin's reins to
the branch of a tree and he
went closer to the tower,
where he found a door.
He tried it but it was locked
tight shut. Looking up,
he realised that there was
no way in except through
the high open window.

13

Suddenly, he heard footsteps on the path and he hid himself in a bush. It was old Ma Gothel and she had a basket over her arm.

Ma Gothel called out, "Rapunzel, Rapunzel, let down your hair."

Ned watched amazed as a long plaited rope of golden hair was lowered to the ground.

Ma Gothel tied the hair around her waist and pulled on it once. She was then slowly lifted up to the tower window.

Ned untied Dobbin and rode home. "So that's where she is," he said to himself. "Why has she been shut away in that tower? The Rapunzel I knew loved being outside."

Chapter 4

The next morning Ned set off through the forest once more. "Let's see if we can get into that tower!" he said, spurring Dobbin on.

When he got to the tower, Ned hid and waited until Ma Gothel had gone. Then Ned stood at the bottom of the tower and called up, "Rapunzel, Rapunzel, let down your hair."

When Rapunzel heard the voice she thought, "That doesn't sound like Ma Gothel." She looked out of the window, but she was too high up to see. So she threaded her plait over the hook beside the window, and let it drop down.

It landed at Ned's feet. He tied it round his waist and tugged the hair once, just as Ma Gothel had done. He was lifted off the ground.

When Rapunzel started to pull on the hair, she thought that whoever it was certainly felt lighter than Ma Gothel. She looked down out of the window again.

Below her, halfway up the tower, someone was holding on to her hair and climbing up – someone smaller than Ma Gothel.

Suddenly, Ned stopped climbing and looked up at the window. "Rapunzel!" he called up. "Is that *you*?"

He was older than Rapunzel remembered, but she recognised who it was straightaway.

"Ned!" she called down. "Is that you?"

Ned braced his feet against the tower and pulled himself up the last few metres.

"Ow!" Rapunzel said, unwinding her hair from the hook.

Ned grinned. "Sorry. So this is where you've been hiding away all this time."

"Not hiding," she said. "I've been hidden – locked away."

"When were you last outside?" Ned asked.

"I can't remember," Rapunzel said. "A long time ago anyway."

"Come out now, come with me," Ned said.

18

"How? The door's locked and Ma Gothel has the only key,"
Rapunzel said. "The window is the only way out, and it's too high for
me to jump."

Ned looked around for a long rope, but there wasn't one.

"Oh Ned, I'm pleased to see you, but you can't stay. Ma Gothel will
soon be back and she mustn't find you here."

So Ned climbed down the tower, using Rapunzel's hair. He promised
to visit her again, and that he'd find a way to free her.

Chapter 5

For the next week, Ned went to the tower every day.
Every day, he'd wait until Ma Gothel had gone out,
and every day he'd stand at the bottom of
the tower and call out, "Rapunzel, Rapunzel,
let down your hair."

But one day, Ned stayed longer
than he should have – too long.
As he was rushing to leave
before Ma Gothel came back,
he forgot his hat.

When Rapunzel saw that Ned
had left his hat, she quickly
hid it in a drawer.
She couldn't let
Ma Gothel find it.

But when Ma Gothel returned, she noticed that
Rapunzel was acting strangely – looking around
the tower nervously and unable to sit still.

Rapunzel had a bedroom at the back of the tower. After she'd gone to bed, Ma Gothel searched the tower.

She looked behind the chairs,

and then she looked behind the bookcase.

Then she looked in the drawers –
and she found Ned's hat.
Someone had got into
the tower!

That night while Rapunzel slept, Ma Gothel cut off most of Rapunzel's hair, so no one else could use it to get into the tower.

When Rapunzel woke the next morning and looked in the mirror, she saw what had happened, and knew that Ma Gothel had somehow found out about Ned. She tried to open her bedroom door, but it was locked.

When Ned arrived at the base of the tower, he called out, "Rapunzel, Rapunzel, let down your hair." But nothing happened.

Ned called out again. This time, the golden plait was lowered out of the window. Ned tied it about his waist as he always did and gave it a pull. Ned noticed that Rapunzel wasn't pulling up the hair as quickly as usual. He looked up at the window above him, but he couldn't see Rapunzel there.

As he got to the window, he heaved himself inside.

Ma Gothel, who'd been hiding below the window, leapt out at Ned.
She had his hat in one hand and the rope of Rapunzel's cut hair
in the other.

Ned jumped back in surprise.

"How dare you come and see *my* Rapunzel behind my back!"
Ma Gothel shrieked.

"She's not *your* Rapunzel," Ned said.
"And you've no right to lock her up
in this tower!"

"My other daughter ran off with
a boy like you, and left me alone.
Rapunzel is happy here with me!"
said Ma Gothel.

"Really? Why don't you ask
Rapunzel what *she* wants?"
Ned asked.

There was a thumping noise
coming from Rapunzel's room.

Ned looked at Ma Gothel.
"I think she's trying to get out,"
he said.

Ma Gothel unlocked Rapunzel's
bedroom door, and pulled
her out.

Rapunzel gasped when she
saw Ned standing in
the tower.

Ma Gothel turned to Rapunzel.
"I treated you with love,
and how have you repaid me?
By meeting this boy behind
my back. Well, now you
have to choose. You can stay
here, with a mother who
loves you, or you can leave
with him."

Rapunzel looked from Ned
to Ma Gothel. She did love
Ma Gothel in a way. After all
the old woman was the only
family she'd ever had, and
Rapunzel didn't want to leave
her on her own. But she didn't
like being locked up in
the tower *and* Ma Gothel had
cut off her hair.

"Keeping me locked up isn't love,"
Rapunzel said. "Cutting off
my hair isn't love."

"Then go!" Ma Gothel shouted.
And she threw the key to
the tower door to Ned.

"I'm sorry," Rapunzel said
to Ma Gothel, and
she turned to Ned.

"Come on," said Ned,
grabbing Rapunzel's
hand and rushing down
the tower steps to
the door. "Let me
take you home –
my home."

They ran down
the spiral stairs,
unlocked the door,
and ran out into
the sunlight.

Ned called Dobbin over and lifted Rapunzel on to the saddle.

Rapunzel looked back at the tower one last time. She could see Ma Gothel leaning out of the window. She was sad to leave Ma Gothel, but she was finally free of the tower.

Ned jumped up behind her and they rode away.

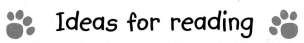

Ideas for reading

Written by Clare Dowdall BA(Ed), MA(Ed)
Lecturer and Primary Literacy Consultant

Learning objectives: infer character's feelings in fiction; empathise with characters and debate moral dilemmas portrayed in texts; use some drama strategies to explore stories or issues

Curriculum links: Citizenship

Interest words: traditional, stammered, braced

Resources: paper and pens

Getting started

This book can be read over two or more reading sessions.

- Show children the front cover. Help them to read the title and blurb. Ask who has heard of this traditional tale, or watched a version of it before.

- Introduce the idea of a traditional tale. List examples that the children know, e.g. *Goldilocks and the Three Bears*. Ask children if they know what the word traditional means, and what a traditional tale might include, e.g. good overcoming bad.

- Look closely at the front cover. Ask children to describe what they can see and how they think Rapunzel might escape from the tower. Discuss how they would feel to be locked in a tower.

Reading and responding

- Read pp2–3 to the children. Ask them to describe the problem that is used to start the story, e.g. that the husband and wife have no money and steal lettuce from Ma Gothel, then to predict what will happen when the man is caught.

- Lead a group reading of pp4–5, where children take on the roles of the narrator, the man, and Ma Gothel. Support children to read aloud with appropriate expression. Discuss whether their predictions were accurate, or whether they were surprised with the outcome.

- Ask children to read to the end of the story. Support them as they read, using questioning to check that they understand the events.